DUST FOR DINNER

story by Ann Turner
pictures by Robert Barrett

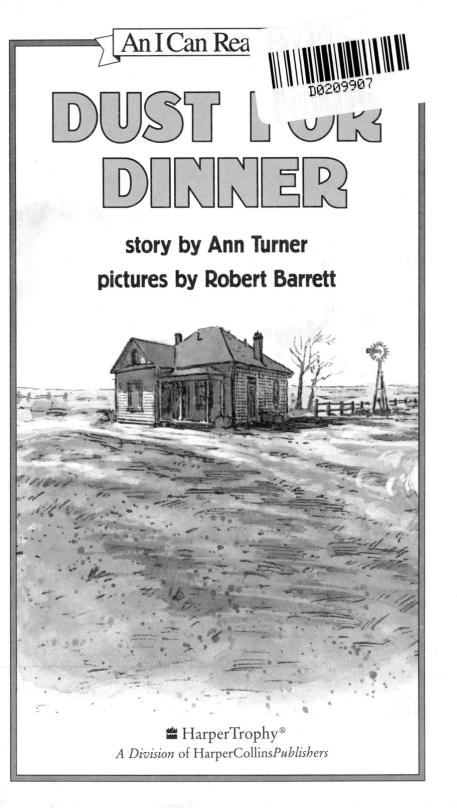

■ HarperTrophy®
A Division of HarperCollins*Publishers*

To all the brave people who
survived the Dust Bowl
—A. T.

For my parents,
Ted and Faye
—R. B.

DUST FOR DINNER
Text copyright © 1995 by Ann Turner
Illustrations copyright © 1995 by Robert Barrett
Printed in the U.S.A. All rights reserved.

Library of Congress Cataloging-in-Publication Data
Turner, Ann Warren.
    Dust for dinner / story by Ann Turner ; pictures by Robert Barrett.
        p.   cm. — (An I can read book)
    Summary: Jake narrates the story of his family's life in the Oklahoma
dust bowl and the journey from their ravaged farm to California during the
Great Depression.
    ISBN 0-06-023376-1. — ISBN 0-06-023377-X (lib. bdg.)
ISBN 0-06-444225-X (pbk.)
    [1. Depressions—1929—Fiction.   2. Family life—Fiction.   3. Farm
life—Fiction.]   I. Barrett, Robert, date, ill.   II. Title.   III. Series.
PZ7.T8535Du   1995   93-34634
[E]—dc20   CIP
                                                                                AC

❖
First Harper Trophy edition, 1997

CONTENTS

1 · DUST STORM

Once we lived in a little house
in a wide place.

Mama had a radio,

and we loved to dance at night.

Papa told me,

"You are growing like a weed, Jake!"

"I'm as tall as our corn," I said.

But one year the rains stopped,

and the wind blew.

We did not listen

to the radio as much,

and we hardly ever danced.

"I wish our wheat grew

as fast as you, Jake," Papa said.

"Where did the rain go?" Maggy asked.

Papa just shook his head.

We looked at the sky and worried.

The wind blew dust

into the house,

and into our faces.

One night I said,

"We are having dust for dinner!"

but nobody laughed.

The next day the sky was dark.

"Listen to that thunder!"

Maggy cried.

The cows ran back and forth.

Sam barked and howled.

"A storm is coming!" Papa shouted.

"Quick! Help me put the animals

in the barn."

"Maggy, don't forget Snowball!"

I said.

Then a black cloud

rolled over the land.

Lightning flashed.

"Run for the house!" Papa yelled.

The dust stung my face.

Papa closed all the windows

and doors,

but the dust still blew inside.

"Nothing stops the dust!"

Mama cried.

She gave us wet cloths

to put over our faces.

The storm sounded like a train

roaring past.

After a long time,

the wind stopped.

"It is all over now," Mama said.

"How can we have a storm

without rain?" Maggy asked.

"It is a storm of dust,

like a black blizzard,"

said Papa.

Mama coughed and said,

"The rains will come back.

Next year will be better."

2 · SOLD!

But the next year

it still did not rain.

The corn and wheat were small.

"The trees look like skeletons,"

Maggy said.

"There is not enough water

to grow a leaf!" I said.

We were afraid.

We had two more dust storms,

and five cows died.

One night Papa said,

"There is no money left.

No crops mean no money."

"Will we have to sell the farm?"

I asked.

"Yes," said Papa, "in an auction,

just like our neighbors."

"Maybe things will be better
in a different place," said Mama.
"Our neighbors went to California,"
said Papa. "We will go, too.
There will be jobs and no dust."
"*No dust in Cal-i-for-ni-ay,*"
Maggy sang, and we smiled.

23

The day of the auction came.

A black car drove up.

"It looks like a funeral,"

I said to Mama.

She grabbed the radio and said,

"Quick, Jake, hide it

in the hayloft.

They can't take our music!"

When I came back,

the man was selling Mama's rocker.

"Sold!" said the man,

and a stranger took it away.

"They are selling Snowball,"
Maggy said, and rubbed her eyes.
"Sold!" the man said,
and Mr. Brown took Maggy's sheep
and our cows away.

Maggy and I went to the hayloft.

"It is not our farm anymore,"
I said sadly.

"We will leave tomorrow."

"At least they did not take
Mama's radio," said Maggy.

"And we still have Sam," I said.

3 · MOVING

The next day we packed.

"They could not take our truck,"

Papa said. "We own that!"

"Jake, get our radio.

They cannot have our music!"

said Mama, and Papa smiled

for the first time that week.

"Jump in, Sam!" Papa said.

Maggy waved good-bye,

but I said,

"Who are you waving to?

Everyone we know lost

their farms and went west."

32

"When we get to California,

will we eat dust for dinner?"

asked Maggy.

Papa shifted gears and shouted,

"No dust in California!"

"*No dust in Cal-i-for-ni-ay!*"

we sang, and

Sam howled on the high notes.

We drove all day.

That night we set up our tent

beside the others near the road.

"Everyone is going west,"

said Mama.

"I miss our house,"

Maggy said softly.

"Me too," I said, and hugged Sam.

We left before the sun came up.

Papa stopped at a farm

down the road.

He and Mama asked,

"Can we milk your cows?

You can pay us with food."

That day they found work.

Other days they did not,

and we had only bread and water

to eat.

"What if Papa cannot find a job in California?" I asked.

"Hush!" said Mama.

"Papa will find a job."

38

That night she said to Papa,

"Maybe it's time to sell our radio."

"Not yet," said Papa.

"I will find something.

Let's wait a little longer."

4 · TROUBLE!

Papa found some work

along the way and

we did not sell the radio.

Three weeks later

Papa stopped the truck

at a big farm.

He knocked on the farmhouse door.

We waited in the truck.

Mama held my hand tight

until Papa came back shouting,

"We have a real job!"

Maggy and I got out and danced.

We laughed and sang,

"She'll be coming

'round the mountain."

The next day

Papa worked in the orchard,

and Mama helped at the big house.

Maggy and I fed the chickens.

"Be good, Sam," I said.

"Don't even look at these chickens!"

That night we had meat for dinner,

and Mama sang to us.

In the morning Papa said,

"Please fix the tent.

The wind took out some pegs."

When we were done

I looked for Sam, but he was gone.

Suddenly, I heard a loud noise.

"Jake, the chickens!"

Maggy cried.

We ran to the chicken yard,

but we were too late.

Sam had a rooster in his mouth.

"Oh, Sam, how could you!"

I cried.

Later Papa said sternly,

"The farmer told me

either the dog goes, or we go."

"How can we let Sam go?"

asked Mama.

"He is all we have left

of our old farm."

Papa had to agree.

Maggy and I sighed.

"Don't worry," Mama said

as she hugged me.

"Papa will find another job."

But Papa and Mama looked worried.

I told Sam, "Papa lost his job,

and it is our fault.

What will we do now?"

5 · A HOUSE

We packed our truck and left.
"We won't stop until we get
to San Francisco," said Papa.
"I hear there are jobs there
and no dust."

We camped outside the city.

"California is crowded," Papa said.

"Everyone wants a job."

"These are hard times for all of us,"
said Mama,

"but you will find something."

Every day Papa looked for a job.

Every night he told us

where he had gone.

Mama made us do lessons

all those long, slow days.

One night Maggy sighed.

"Will we ever live in a house again?"

"Hush," said Mama.

"Things will get better."

"When?" Maggy asked,

but Mama just looked stern.

Then one day Papa came home

and said, "Sweets for the sweet!

I have a job!

I will be a watchman at a big store."

He hugged us and gave us cookies.

Even Sam got one.

"Will we have a house?"

asked Maggy.

"We will have a house,"

said Papa.

Mama said,

"And we will have music!"

We packed up our truck

for the last time.

Other people looked at us.

They wished they had a job, too.

Papa drove to a house
with blue shutters.
"Oh!" cried Maggy.
"There is a tree with leaves."
"And there is no dust," I said.

Mama set up the radio on the table.

A sweet, sad song came out.

"Lord, I'm going down this road

feeling bad . . . "

"It is about us," I said.

"It is about hard times,"
said Papa.

"And traveling," Maggy said.

"And still being together,"
said Mama.

We hugged each other for a long time
at the end of the song.

Sam lifted his nose and howled.

"He knows we are home now,"
said Mama,
and we smiled.

AUTHOR'S NOTE

In the 1930's, winds stripped soil from the dry field of parts of Texas, Oklahoma, Kansas, Colorado, an New Mexico—an area that became known as the Du Bowl. Strong winds blew the soil into thick, whirlin clouds of dust that terrified people and animals an ruined property. People ran for their houses and pu wet cloths over their mouths so they could breathe. animals were caught in the dust storms, they sometime suffocated.

These storms happened for several reasons. Becaus there was hardly any rain at that time, the soil was fin and dry. Trees died, grass withered, and roots dried u so there was nothing to hold down the soil. Farmer did not know how to plow their fields a special wa so the dust would not blow away.

Since farmers could not live off the land anymor their homes and land were sold—or taken back by th bank—to pay off their debts. Many from the Dust Bow fled to California to try and find jobs. Some foun work as poorly paid workers on big farms.

The terrible drought didn't end until the rain came after 1941. The government ordered farmers t plant shelterbelts of trees to protect the land. Contou plowing helped keep the soil from blowing away.

Many of the families who went to California neve did find a better life and remained poor farmworker But some families, like Jake and Maggy's, did find ne jobs and a life not threatened by dust storms.

64